Reflections from the Heart

Poem & Memories

Gladine P. Bruer
&
Family and Friends

PROISLE PUBLISHING

© COPYRIGHT 2024 BY GLADINE P. BRUER

ISBN: 978-1-963735-04-8

All rights reserved. No part of this book may be reproduced or transmitted in any form or by any means, electronic or mechanical, including photocopying, recording, or by any information storage and retrieval system, without permission in writing from the copyright owner.

The views expressed in this work are solely those of the author and do not necessarily reflect the views of the publisher, and the publisher disclaims any responsibility for them.

To order additional copies of this book, contact:

Proisle Publishing Services LLC
39-67 58th Street, 1st floor
Woodside, NY 11377, USA
Phone: (+1 646-480-0129)
info@proislepublishing.com

DEDICATION

Deotha Neeley
Leona Armstead
Cecilia Alice Bruer
Maggie Muse Jones
Betty Pitts Brown
Georgette Barber
Ethel Moore
Ruth (Drewery) Lewis

Ladies who believe in The Lord and Themselves

ACKNOWLEDGEMENTS

Book cover design by
Denitra Bruer-Robinson
Edited by Cathy Stutler

SISTERS SHARING AND CARING

Leona Pannell Herbert
Deotha Davidson Pannell
Denitra Lynn Bruer-Robinson
Maryland Mosley
Sandra Sweeney-Edmonds
Carmen Gore
Jackie (Drewery) Bruer
Gail Revels
Alice Jolla
Sandy Peters
Josette Saunders
Angela Mayfield-Brown
Jackie Cosby-Lawson
Pia Edmonds
Cherie Franklin
Alice Robinson-Sanders
Shari L. Collias
Crystal Goode
Cathy Stutler
Sabrena Olive Gillis
Susan Cannon-Ryan

Chennel Bruer
Shirley Roberts
Shirley (Brown) Armstead
Jenee Brown
Jence Brown
Ellen Toliver
Judy Gillenwater
Judie Hall
Anna Doreas (MaMa Anna)
Silvana Bruer
Beverly Doreas-Gwen Jackson
Leanna Hill
Joyce Savolia
Ivin Lee
Mary Booker
Ruth Booker
Linda Cosby
Shirley (Howzie) Hutcherson
Willa Bell Plantin

Eunice Kineaid
Ruth Jone
Phyllis Toliver
Sherron Jones
Janet Lawson
Gloria (Jones) Davison
Oretha Hicks
Karen Davison-Foster
Janice (Robinson) Knight
Mary (Calloway) Armstead
Renae (Lee) Pannell
Angel Mosley
Cindy Lawson
Fran (Howzie) Harris
Jane Diggs
Dr. Julie DeTemple
Kay Teufel
Dr. Kristie Hensley
Veanis Russel
Wadie Gant
C. Wesley

Gayle Manchin	Jean Brown	Bonita Perry-Dean
Bonnie Brown	Barbara Waller	Loretta Jet-Haddad
Jewell Mitchell	Ann Waller	Roz Ellis & Mama Hazel
Mary Darnell	Kathy Price	Reba Higginbotham
Becky Frazier	Jamilia Price	Annette Vaung White
Darlene Green	Tomikah Paige	Deb Staple
Marlene Hackett	Janice Mosley	Pat Harris
Hazel Wooster	Shirley (Greene) Lyles	Lola Harris
Dr. J. Lee	Lavetta McKnight	Charline Bennett
Shirley Womack	Lisa Miller	Hazel Gardley
Elain Ricks	Christie Day-Shavers	Nicki Burgess
Teddy Mayfield	Ms. Mattie Day	D J Johnson
Dorothy Price	Carolyn Faucett	Cher Taylor
Carrie Erby	Pam Watts	Vonnie Herbert
Lorraine (White) Smith	Mrs. Carolyn Tinney (CEF)	Stephanie Bruer
Ernestine (Booker) Cooper	Ruby Brown (sister)	Sleika Henderson
Ruby Chapell	Towanda Bryant	Tootsie Coleman
Ruth (Lawson) Henderons	Della Pannell-Milner	Renae Miller
Karen (Booker) Joyce	Barbara (Davidson) Issa	Lisa Bruer
Libby Booker	April Davison	Judy Sorgman
Anna Gilmer	Laverne Davison	Anne Waller
Cleota Thacker (Mama T)	Lorraine Roberts	Silvana Drum
Margaret Bruer	Willa M. Jolia	Ana Lledo
		Sherrie Bausely

All of my Sisters at The Charleston,
West Virginia Women's Club
Thanks for being a part of my life.
-Gla

TABLE OF CONTENTS

Introduction	
Making Friends — Short Story	1
Watching You — Poem	3
Smile, God Loves You	
Short Story by Janice Robinson Knight	4
Inner Peace — Poem	11
Mama Anna — Poem	12
I Think I'm Feeling Better Already	
Short Story by Karen (Davidson) Foster	14
God First —- Poem	16
Breathless — Poem	17
Reflections of my Life	
Short Story by Gloria (Jones) Davidson	19
Memories (To GranMa Nonie) — Poem	21
Well Done! — Poem	22
Where Shall I Be? — Poem	24
Strengthening the Value of Differences in People	
Short Story by Christabel Danby-Cabbina	25
Miss Ruth — Poem	
(In Remembrance of Mrs. Ruth Bias (Drewery) Lewis)	27
D — Poem	28
My Naomi — Poem	29
One Body - Multiple Identities	
Short Story by Denitra Bruer-Robinson	30
Inspired by an Image (Granny Neeley) — Poem	34
Little Fella's — Poem	35

By Chance — Poem	37
A Cold Man in Your Day — Poem	38
I Adore — Poem by Brittany White	39
Days Gone By — Poem	40
The Smile of an Empty Face — Poem	41
Are You Unhappy? — Poem	42
Red's Daughter	
Poem by Crystal (Armstead) Good	43
Pass You By (My Favorite) — Poem	45
LIFE — Poem	46
The Moore You Want — Poem	47
Pages of Your Life	
Poem (Taken from the Wordless Book)	48
Ms. Hicks — Poem	50
Baby Boy! — Poem	51
Family — Poem	52

INTRODUCTION

Reflections from the Heart is a book filled with expression of feelings from the hearts of so many women whose paths I have crossed in my lifetime, be it the past, present or the future agenda.

The short stories and poems within this book are truly inspiring thoughts and sayings that have helped to support the positive causes to nurture and develop the minds of so many—mentoring, sisterhood, togetherness, mental aid, health and strength of our fellow sisters that we would like to share. Reason being: the Lord wants us to care for each other and to shelter the lost and to comfort the unsettled, so read and enjoy the heartfelt moments that are in this book with Blessings from God.

Always,
Gla

Reflections of the Heart
MAKING FRIENDS
SHORT STORY

It was a warm summer afternoon and Manzee the mouse was sitting alone on his Nana's front porch trying to attract a friend or two. He was just visiting and didn't know anyone in the neighborhood.

Manzee was the big man in his neighborhood, the kids would say Manzee couldn't be beat as a friend and helper in every way. But he was on a new and different turf, so Manzee needed some ideas for making friends. He sat and thought for a few minutes, and a light bulb lit up in his head. *I know, I'll build a train and I'll ask the two little guys next door to help me. We will collect wood, get nails, and a hammer from Nana to complete the job.* Manzee jumped off the porch and trotted over to the house next door knocking on the door and asking the two little boys, Anthony and Antjuan, to help him build the train from scrap materials.

Anthony and Antjuan were more than delighted to help, Antjuan wanted to make sure the train had a bell to ring, so he went to his Papa's to make sure the train had a bell to ring, so he went to his Papa's tool shed and retrieved an old bell, Anthony collected all the wood he could find, and Manzee got the hammer and nails. Manzee didn't want to appear to be taking the lead, so he gave Antjuan and Anthony a chance to bolt the wood pieces together to make each piece fit perfectly, then they set up the homemade tracks, so the train could go around and around.

Every kid in the neighborhood heard about the train and the work of the three newfound friends and wanted to play also, so a pack of kids ran over to Nana's and they took turns playing with the new toy. No one clashed or had any disagreements, everyone enjoyed playing together and finding new friends and adventure in each other.

"Boy!" said Manzee, "I'll always remember this day because I've found new friends and learned the importance of being part of a team working together." Manzee always got excited when he was told he was going to Nana's, he knew he would see his new friends and spend some quality time with the new Rat Pack on Nana's block.

Reflections of the Heart

Anthony and Antjuan would always be so excited to see Manzee and visit with him. They always had new and great ideas together as a team.

The train was a symbol of groups traveling in the same direction, to have togetherness, love, and enjoyment of all, and with the entire neighborhood joining in, made it so fulfilling and adventurous to all involved, to show how communicating and sharing ideas and thoughts can be so valuable to the hearts, souls, and minds of all.

Friends and teamwork make for such nice memories, so Manzee will have this time as happy, bright, and beautiful thoughts of time while growing up. Friends until the end!

<u>*Reflections of the Heart*</u>
WATCHING YOU

Watching you grow up so fine
Makes me smile just all the time
I think of all the fun we've had
And boy it makes me oh so glad
To know that we still have some time
And here I am near my prime
Life can be oh so nice
When you can get one big slice
A smile, a laugh, a cry or two
I cherish these I've had with you
And now you will get your turn
To Live, To Love, and also Learn
That children are a GOD send
This I offer friend to friend
As I close with pleasant thoughts
You're on my mind and in my mind
A blessed addition to our world
Whether it be Boy or Girl????
Will just give my Life another Whirl
Love Forever
Mommy!!!!!!

This Poem is dedicated to my daughter
Denitra Lynn Bruer-Robinson
06/27/2006
GPB (Gladine Parnell Bruer)
Thanks for being You.

Reflections of the Heart

SMILE, GOD LOVES YOU
SHORT STORY BY
JANICE ROBINSON KNIGHT

"The day Gladine Bruer sent me this journal, I now have the opportunity to share some of the most important (memorable) events (past and present) in my life!

Thanks, Gla
for including me in *Reflections from the Heart.*"

PAST 03/08/69

The day my son, Corey, was born, I said he was going to be very special—just had no idea how special. He was almost perfect at birth, I just wasn't ready for the cryin'.

I tried to breastfeed and was unsuccessful and Corey wanted "milk" now.

As a child, my life was filled with fun times, but then there were not-so-fun times. My mother was very firm and strict (most especially about her girls). Growing up, I can remember my mother working (short-order cook) and bringing home something special for us when she returned home. What comes to mind is the day she brought home a wonderful cheeseburger which I was privileged to have on my own (without sharing this time), and I thought it would be the best burger. However, the burger had a real funny taste to it, and I eventually threw it away. Now, as I look back, I suspect there was probably nothing wrong with the burger, but because I was such a picky eater, my mother called herself bringing home something special for me. We did laugh about it some days later. It was a real let-down when I couldn't eat that burger.

Once, when me and my brother were very young (between the ages of five and eight years old), I told a lie on him. Jerome used to wet the bed, and we had to share a bed together. On this particular time, the wetting of the bed must have rubbed off on me. I can remember dreaming that I was up and using the toilet and I, in turn, wetted the bed. But as children sometimes do, I didn't want to accept the responsibility that it was me – not Jerome – who wetted the bed this time. Well, needless to say, Jerome got a whipping (after a while, I felt bad that I told the lie on him) and he was really upset. He knew that it was not him this time, but he also knew that my mother was not going to believe him, especially after she had already whipped him. I told myself after that I wouldn't do that again – lie on him. And, I believe that I kept my word to me!

During elementary school, I had been bullied by a girl who could "throw down" as they said back then, and I was quite scared of fighting. However, on the day tat this girl (Nancy) beat me up, I went home crying. Well, needless to say, my mother didn't believe in you getting your butt whipped without you trying to fight back. So I received a whipping from my mother, and was escorted back to the school grounds to find Nancy, and confronted her and we began the fight all over again. This time – guess what – I won! And, I won because I did not want to receive another whipping from my mother. After this incident of fighting, there were two other fights during my school years. I lost one to a boy who hit me in the stomach, and won the other with a girl who had been bullying me. Oh well, such is life!

High School was a real transition, as I felt awkward and not *in* with the 'in crowd.' I soon got over that feeling. In the 12th grade, I decided to skip school that day, but got caught as my boyfriend went and told my mother. She came and got me, and I was about to wet my pants. However, my mother told me that I didn't have to skip school. If I didn't want to go, just stay home. This was the smartest move my mother could have made – I think she used psych on me. As a result, I never skipped another day.

My first trip to California was a real eye-opener, and when I got off the bus, I was pretty scared. There were real hippies, which I had not seen on this order. As I waited for my friend to pick me up, I was so frightened by some of the sights that I saw, I stayed in one place, and almost forgot that I needed to go to the bathroom. Well, by the time my friend arrived to pick me up, I ran to the car and was almost hysterical. After only a few days in sunny California, I calmed down and began to see such a diversity of people, that it was almost too exciting and overwhelming. During my time in California, I became almost a 'wild woman.' The parties never cease, and there is always someplace to go and something to do. Never a dull moment for me. In fact, I burned myself out in California. I worked Monday through Thursday, and when Thursday evening arrived, the party began and continued until Sunday night. Needless to say, my body was taking a toll, and I became ill. They wanted to give me surgery, but I was not comfortable in having surgery there, and called my mother to ask if I could come home to have the surgery in Michigan. Being the mother that she was, she allowed me to return home.

The day I found out that I was truly pregnant. At first (even after the doctor told me) I didn't believe it. I never became big in the stomach until the end of my seventh month going into my eighth month. So to me, it really wasn't true. However, in the eighth month, when I awoke from sleep, I saw and knew that I had a life growing on the inside of me. All I could think of was that I wanted this baby to be healthy with ten fingers, toes, eyes, ears, and none and all the limbs to be in perfection the way God designed them to be. As this life began to grow in me, then the questions began to bombard me: what would the baby look like, be like, and would I be able to provide for this child and give them the love they needed or required.|? At the time, I didn't feel like I would be a good mother. It was pretty memorable, in that many things that I worried about before Corey (my son) arrived on the scene, were truly unnecessary.

The day I received the Lord Jesus Christ as my personal savior (October, 1983), my life (on the inside) truly did change. I didn't know how much until the day I witnessed a former boyfriend who told me to get out of his house, and that if I didn't change back to the Janice he knew, he did not want me to ever come around. My response was shock and laughter – I thought he was kidding. Not the case. Not the case. Then as I left his house, I suddenly realized that I had been rejected and the funny thing was that I didn't feel bad for the first time in my life with rejection. I had a knowing on the inside that my life truly had changed (and for the better I must say).

Reflections of the Heart

I received total healing in my body (from believing what the Lord Jesus Christ did for me on Calvary) two years after I was born again. In the past, I dealt with a lot of medical issues (three surgeries in my stomach), and I was told by two doctors that I would always have trouble with my back. Well, I went on a quest and found a scripture in Isaiah 53:7 which says "by His stripes I '**was**' healed", and then in 1 Peter 2:24 it says "by His stripes I '**were**' healed**.**" Then I asked the Lord in prayer that if this was true what it says in the Word of God, that I would no longer have to suffer with the back nor female problems as I had in the past. I once had spinal meningitis and the doctors had given up on me recovering (but God had other plans for me). But on this day, after receiving my healing, by believing and confessing what the Word of God said – I knew that I did not have to ever suffer from back problems (nor female problems) as I did in the past. Now the thing that I had to continue to learn was that I must confess the Word every day. Because, when I slacked off saying this – the enemy came and hit my body with a pain that buckled my knees and I fell down and asked God to help me. After crying for about an hour. I heard the voice of the Lord in my spirit saying "You are healed. Why did you stop saying what I said in my word?" I'm not sure why I stopped, but I started that very moment, and eventually got up from the floor (and the pain was gone) and made my way to the church service that evening. From that moment unto this day, I continue to confess that by Jesus' stripes, I am healed!

The day I was nominated for the prestigious Dr. Martin Luther King recognition award at Dow Corning Corporation (January 2000), I was truly surprised! A mentor, who had tutored me on some politics of the corporate ways, submitted my name, which I was almost in disbelief because this was not a norm for her. During our times together, I would share with her some of the community activities I was involved in – never thinking she would use this – because most of the activities involved some pretty amazing things that were happening. In any event, at the awards ceremony, it was the first time my mother, husband and few other family members visited me at my work site. I was truly thankful and godly proud that they were there with me. I did not think that I deserved this award, but I humbled myself and accepted and received what only God could have done for me. My mother seemed to be overly proud as I looked at her with a smile on her face, and such a gleam in her eyes, and then she gave me this truly big (and tight) hug – I enjoyed every moment of it.

October, 2001, I was accepted as a Volunteer at the Covenant Harrison Hospital in Saginaw, MI. My mission was to 'cuddle' babies that needed additional love and tender loving care. Prior to being accepted as a 'cuddler' it was a desire of 10 years before this time to be what I termed as 'bonding' Little did I know that the 10-year desire would come to pass, and that I would become a 'cuddler'. The first baby I held, it felt awkward – it had been over 30 years basically since I held such a little one, and given the responsibility of feeding, burping, and ensuring that the baby was getting the right amount of oxygen. Initially, I was thinking that I would be with the normal newborn babies, but God had other plans – I would become a cuddler in the Neo-Natal Unit with the preemie babies. What an honor and privilege. I get to, not only hold these little ones, but I'm also afforded the opportunity to pray over them, sing to them, and tell them what a beautiful creation God made when He designed them. I get so much pleasure out of this activity, that sometimes I'm overwhelmed with such joy for these little ones. And, I'm not willing to give this day and time up for anything (other than commitments with and for my husband, child, or family members)

Corey's first day of school. First of all, I really was apprehensive about letting him go to school by himself (I wonder if other parents have some of these apprehensions – Ha). I knew that I had prepared him, but I was a bit reluctant in letting him go off to school by himself. He did just fine, and told me so many things that happened on that day that I was just amazed. He talked so much, until I had to leave the room for a breather. Whew! There was a lot he had to tell me.

End of elementary school (6th grade) and first dance. I was one of the chaperones, and it was quite uncomfortable for Corey (and I must admit, me too) to have his mother present. Especially with the girl he had taken to the dance. I decided to step outside to give him a breather, and when I returned, he was dancing with the girl (Carmen) he had taken to the dance. It was quite a sight to see Corey can dance, and he was pretty good if I have to say so (this is probably a mother's bias).

During elementary school, there were some girls that liked Corey (you know how that goes with girl-boy thing). Well, on one occasion, these girls ran Corey home because one of them wanted a kiss, and another one wanted to fight. Corey came running in the house, panting and laughing, and I was wondering what had happened. Well those girls stood outside my door, waiting for Corey to come out – he didn't, but I did. I told them that they had better get home, unless they wanted me to take them home and tell their mothers what had been done. Needless to say, (girls were different then) they ran off. Corey, later told me that he didn't want to fight the girls. And I commended him for that. However, I must admit that I told him if a girl persisted in pestering and/or hitting him that his first course of action was to tell the principal/teacher. If that didn't work, push the girl down and then walk away. If that didn't work, tell me the girl's name and where she lived and I would go and speak to the parents. I tried to encourage Corey not to fight girls, but at the same time, protect yourself as best as you can. Needless to say, Corey only had to push one girl down during elementary school. Whew! I was glad

Junior High school was quite a transition, as the peer pressure was on. I was then put on a spot to try and keep up with the "Jones." Well, I had to inform my son of the reality that I was not going (and could not) keep up with the "Jones" However, Corey had a godfather (Thomas Malone–deceased) who was very generous to my son and provided him with some of those things that I could not afford. This young man was quite pleased – to say the least!

During elementary school, Corey fell during a basketball game, and chipped his front tooth, He was pretty good at basketball (now remember, this is a mother being biased). He was so devastated that he couldn't stare at the mirror for the next two days. After the incident, until I could get him to the dentist, he wouldn't smile. Oh boy, after the dentist's visit, I couldn't get him to quit grinning. I never saw such a grin on a person as it was on Corey that day. He was so happy that his tooth was fixed, and that he could smile again. Guess what, I was glad for him too!

INNER PEACE

Cool ripples of water in a stream
Gives me Inner Peace
An inspirational Book to read
Gives me Inner Peace
Thoughts of God's Word
Gives me Inner Peace
Focusing on Peace within
Thoughts That are Good
Not of sin
Inner Peace restores the should
Inner Peace
My Ultimate Goal!!!

Gladine Pannell Bruer – March 20, 2007

MAMA ANNA
DEDICATED TO A LADY WHO IMPACTED MY LIFE IN SO MANY WAYS

A lady of love

A lady of kindess

A lady with class

Who\s been a part of my past

Always with a smile on her face

I could always enjoy her in any place

At church – at Fellowship and even the mall

Oh Mama Anna, we had a ball!!!

I will always remember the wisdom she shared

I will always know that she really cared

So lay your head down and get your rest

Because we all know God picks only the best

So Mama Anna, I won't say goodbye

And I will try real hard not to cry

I'll just throw you a kiss with a smile and a sigh

As my Mama Anna goes to heaven on high!!

Anna (Stovall) Dorcas 5-6-2000
(G. Bruer) May 2007

KAREN (DAVIDSON) FOSTER

Karen, my dearest cousin, was one of the first to return her journal – stumped for words, she had no clue where she wanted to start. To tell of any part of her life – but once she got to writing, she decided to share her healthy habits with us. Starting with GOD as the main ingredient. Which she had made very clear that she was feeling better already with him in her Life.

Reflections of the Heart

I THINK I'M FEELING BETTER ALREADY

BY KAREN (DAVIDSON) FOSTER

It took me a long time to decide on what to write. I finally started writing, clueless of what to say and of course it depended on the day or my mood, it can set the tone of what I want to talk about. At first, I wanted to talk about my physical ailments and what all I've done to get myself feeling good again, but I think that's just about everybody else's story. So instead, I decided to build healthy habits into my lifestyle to:

1 - Reduce Stress – by saying NO and not feeling bad about it.

2 - Incorporate Exercise

3 - Better eating habits

4 -Positive Thinking

> I'm feeling better already. The prime ingredient that I've incorporated into my Life is God.

My most memorable moment was when I visited Miami Beach, Florida – the water, the beach and the beautiful homes on the water. Maybe one day I'll live in one of those homes. I've always aspired to own my own business or become an inventor and profit from the idea, neither has happened yet for various reasons. However, I'll always remember what my Aunt Alice told me – she said "You will know when you are ready." I think I'm getting close.

Another memorable moment was when my daughter Stephanie signed her letter of intent to go to college on a full scholarship to Florida A&M University a (HBCU) Historically Black College and University, to play Women's Basketball. The trip was very enlightening in that it showed me and my husband (Steve) how misinformed we were about HBCUs. The atmosphere was rich with culture, excitement, inspiring and full of Life. I wish I had such an opportunity, but Glory to God and all of our Trailblazers who paved the way to make this all possible.

In the past I have been sooooooo busy that I never took the time for myself, not remembering a lot of the activities had done with or attended with my children so I started keeping a diary in 1999. It hasn't stopped me from being busy, but it does help me remember my past and you know what – it makes me feel better to know that I have a life and so much to share. That's why I know I'm feeling better already.

GOD FIRST

As life that pass with such great haste
Time for salvation we do waste
In need of food or water your thirst
Always remember
GOD FIRST
You wake up to the morning Glory
Before the day ends – you have a story
Light of day and dark of night
GOD FIRST
Or Life just ain't right
Do your best – not your worst
Remember to keep
GOD FIRST!!!

Gladine Pannell Bruer
03/20/2007

BREATHLESS

As the air stands still
And the days passed swiftly
The weather, it changes
Sunshine to Rain
Take a deep breath of the World we are living in
Define it, Look at it, embrace it
Be thankful for it
Think about it
In the End you are just Breathless!!!

By – Gla
To – The World
May 2006

GLORIA (JONES) DAVIDSON

My Aunt forever these are her heartfelt feelings and she is so gracious to share as always

Reflections of the Heart

REFLECTIONS OF MY LIFE

To My Niece, Gla, who I love, admire and respect.

In my journal, I have chosen to reflect on a few of my heartfelt memories. Thank you for this opportunity. I am looking forward to reading Sisters from the Heart. God bless you and keep you safe always.

Love – Aunt Gloria
February 2, 2006

CHILDHOOD
Elementary – Junior High – High School

After soul searching and reflecting on my life, I realized early on that my journey is part of God's plan for me.

God is and always has been the head of my life in all things.

My first memorable heartfelt reflections as a child. My family relocated from Atlanta, Georgia to Charleston, West Virginia. I was seven years old. Met a neighbor girl who was six years old. Through the years, we formed a special bond with one another that is unbreakable.

We started elementary school together. Graduated high school together.

Before leaving Charleston, West Virginia to get married, she was with child. I told her then that her baby would be born on my birthday. "You guessed it" She gave birth on my birthday, July 26. We have been friends for 65 years, looking forward to many more.

Living miles apart never affected our friendship or our sisterly love for each other. We are truly sisters from the heart.

MARRIAGE

I am blessed to be married for 51 years to a great husband and friend. We were High School sweethearts. Out of this union, God blessed us with four wonderful children. I am eternally grateful for my children. They are the greatest gifts I could have ever wished for. I was told by my doctors after my first child was born, I would never have another child. Praise God, he had other plans for my life. God knew I had much love to give. He decided to bless us with three more children.

Through it all, with God's love, grace, and wisdom, even though it was not always easy, we have always prevailed with much prayer.

We have four grown children, six grandchildren, and one great-grandchild. We are a family that truly loves each other. Always trying to do what we can for others. I sincerely hope and pray, as a family, we have been and continue to be an example to others.

My sisters – listen to your children. Never fail to tell them *I love you* no matter what, these three words are priceless.

And now, these three remain – faith, hope and love. But greatest of these is Love. 1 Corinthians 13:13

CELEBRATION OF LOVE

August 2004, my husband and I celebrated our 50th Wedding Anniversary. It was a joyous occasion, given by our children and family members. We had a beautiful celebration. We renewed our vows at our church by our pastor. In attendance were our family, church family and friends. Following the ceremony, there was a reception for our church family.

Later that same evening, a reception of celebration was given for our family and friends. This was, by far, one of the most heartfelt celebrations in my life. Family and friends, children, sisters, brothers, nieces, nephews, cousins, in-laws, and friends, sharing moments from our past and present relationships. We had great home-cooked meals and desert. All prepared by family members. The facilities where this celebration was held was beautiful.

We appreciate and love our family and friends for taking time from their busy lives to travel and participate in this celebration of love with us. God bless you all.

Reflections of the Heart
MEMORIES

Memories I do recall
Memories remember all
Good ones – bad ones – sad ones too
Memories, they are all of you
Memories from dusk to dawn
Memories, they linger on
Memories to cry and laugh
Memories bring back the Past
Memories I can't forget
Memories to me you left
Memories full of tears – laughter – and a smile
Memories with every mile
Memories forever there
Memories, you're everywhere
Memories I see your Face
Memories you're in my space
Memories I cherish much
Memories of your soft touch
Memories, I do declare
Memories of you
Will always be There!!!

By Gla
To Granma Nonie
5-2006

Reflections of the Heart
WELL DONE!

As we enter into this world
Little boy or little girl
Not knowing any of the fads
Not even knowing Mom or Dad
Look around, all is strange
Boy is your life about to change
No more closeness to mama's breast
You think you will pass the Test?
Trials, Truths and manmade gadgets
Movie Stars and Beauty Pageants
Money, richest and material things
Fur coats, clothes and diamond rings
Oh the temptations this life brings
Lord, you will be wanting everything
But among the abundance of so much sorrow
Will you be able to face tomorrow?
With hunger, poverty and war
Lord knows who is keeping score
Just be thankful for the Father's son
Who made our lives a Holy one.
To sin, to error and be forgiven
While on this earth are we really living?
Respect, are we giving to one another
To Mom, Dad, Sister and Brother
What have we contributed to mankind?
Deep down in our hearts what will one find?
As days, weeks, months, and years pass on
And you days on earth have made the run
While looking at the stars, moon, sky and the sun
What will they say?

WELL DONE?

By Gla
To All my family and friends
5-2006

WHERE SHALL I BE?

As I gaze out into the Trees
I ask myself *Where Shall I be?*
I wonder down the path of life
Thinking about the world's hard strife
The daughter role I've played that part
Remembering my mother's heart
Sister, I'll always cherish
For her love, it just flourish
Wife, I guess I am okay
I kept my mind from day to day
Mother, now that's a spot
Being strong it takes a lot
Life, it opens doors you see
That's why I ask
Where Shall I Be????

By Gla
5-2006

Reflections of the Heart

STRENGTHENING THE VALUE OF DIFFERENCES IN PEOPLE
BY DANBY-CABBINA, CHRISTABEL
SOUTH CHARLESTON, WV 25309

INTRODUCTION

Everyone has their differences, but I use these differences to better understand people. At school, I respect others whether they are different than me or closely similar. If anyone asks for help, I always try to give them a hand. I also have been able to communicate with others through listening, which in turn will benefit me in the future. I hope the things I do and learn from others' differences will make me a better person and help others be one too.

The different people I encounter teach me so much about their culture, religion, and race. Being young, I like to learn new things about everything so when I get the chance to take that opportunity, I don't waste it. During school, som kids were uncomfortable with other kids, but after getting to know them, we found out so much about them and were eager to learn more about others. At other time, I might have met someone and used the knowledge I have learned to understand and help them. Now is the time to embrace these values and differences so we can all have a better understanding of people.

STRENGTHENING THE VALUE OF DIFFERENCES IN PEOPLE

Differences are what make us unique. The American Heritage dictionary of English language defines differences as the degree or amount by which things differ. My definition of differences is the certain aspect or quality that distinguishes us from one another. The way one can strengthen the value of differences in others is to appreciate the quality or aspect that makes us who we are. To value someone is to know their worth, a quality that demands admiration and respect. We should always try to emphasize how grateful we are for the hard work and efforts by our community leaders. I take an active role in my community by serving as a Hope Youth Leader and an active member of my local congregation.

As a Hope Youth Leader, I spend a lot of my time getting to know my peers. Through communication and understanding, I get to learn what's on the minds of my fellow students; like their hopes, and fears for the future. There are over three hundred youths in the Hope program, as a leader it is my job to plan and organize activities that would benefit my peers. Last year, I hosted a Teen Summit for the Hope program. In the program, I selected a panel of teens and then asked them what some of their biggest issues were. The discussions lead to new ideas and many other possibilities to consider. The Hope program has given me the strength to set my sights higher, it has opened my mind to a world of possibilities and opportunities.

As a member of my congregation, I attend meetings three days a week and participate in the local preaching work. To be an active member in my congregation, I prepare for assigned talks and sudy on a weekly basis. My congregation has made me stronger, compassionate and sensible: it has also taught me the way of righteousness and has helped me to become a good-willed citizen.

There are a lot of people in my community I look up to and one day hope to be like. Their strength empowers and inspires me to become something greater. Sometimes it is easy to forget the sacrifices they have made in order to benefit the community. I know it takes time and, in many instances, money that these individuals are willing to give for the good of the community.

My life has been enhanced by many people. Everyday people – like my classmates who help me go through my school days with ease and determination– teachers and administration –who willingly give their advice and council– and congregation members –who wouldn't hesitate for a minute to help with any issues I may go through.– I also want to thank the hard-working individuals of the Hope staff who would stop at nothing to help a child by paving the way for their future. In conclusion, I would like to give utmost thanks to my mother and father. They have made me what I am today.

Reflections of the Heart

MISS RUTH
IN REMEMBRANCE OF JACKIE'S MOM
MRS. RUTH BIAS (DREWERY) LEWIS
EXIT 6-28-2006

She's now at peace and gone to Rest

After being put to the Test

The test she has Passed

In heaven at Last

So remember her Well

With all the memories you can Tell

Her smile, Her Laugh and her Advice

Would make you think more than Twice

With her thoughts, her voice, and her expression

You knew you were in for True Confession

So with these thoughts, of all it's Truth

We will never forget

Miss Ruth!!!

Gladine Pannell Bruer
7-3-2006

D

D-My one and only girl
A breath of sunshine in my world.
D-termined to pass every test
D-my daughter, she's the best
D-sire to respect and love all
D-Four foot/11 but stand so Tall
D-serving of so many things
D-cide to take what life will bring
D-lightful as a song you sing
D-she is my everything

By Gla
To Denitra
5-2006

MY NAOMI

As I gaze into her big brown eyes
I see peace, happiness, love
I see the Big smile on her face
I hear the beat of her heart – pacing
I feel her every thought, her every breath
She's so peaceful, enjoyable, pleasant loyal
She's awesome
She will always be My Joy!!!
My Naomi!!!

Love to my Naomi

10-2006
GPB

Reflections of the Heart

ONE BODY – MULTIPLE IDENTITIES
BY DENITRA BRUER-ROBINSON

I am a middle class, African-American female. Every day I face living at the intersections of race, class, and gender. I know that my life is one of both privilege and oppression, because I have experienced both. My face, for example, has brought more oppression than privilege.

I was 9 years old when I first realized the down-side of being black in America. I went to try out for cheerleading mascot, and they had already decided to pick a little white girl. I was undoubtedly better, so they just decided not to take any mascot. Cheerleading really opened my eyes to racism. Twice in the elementary school and all-star leagues, I was initially told I had second best score. Then after decision for captain were made, I was told that "OOPS" you really had the highest score. In my junior high and high school years, I always received the highest scores in cheerleading try-outs, but the sponsor would make a white girl captain over me. The sponsor's reason was that she did not feel I was a leader. That was bullcrap because I was student body president, and I also made up the squad's cheer routines. To this day, that pisses me off because I knew I was the best, and evey one else knew it too. In junior high, I was choreographing routines for high school teams, and by the end of high school, I was a three-time All-American cheerleader, I was definitely the best. If my skin was white, the outcomes would have been different. Being overlooked hurt, but it made me work that much harder, and want to be that much better. My competitiveness flowed over into my academic endeavors.

I have always chosen courses which are challenging, and I excel. Upon entering high school, the guidance counselor asked me if my parents agreed with me taking advanced classes. That is nonsense. Evidently, some people have preconceived stereotypes that black people are unintelligent and backwards.

My skin color has also caused me to be refused a hotel room. It is ridulous, all money is green, and business should be business. When I go into stores, I get tired of being constantly eyed and followed by salespeople and security guards. As time went on, I grew more defensive as a result of these experiences. I have experienced the flip-side of Peggy McIntosh's accounts of white privilege. When I am told about national heritage or about "civilization," I am shown that white people made it what it is. I know that in history, whites made blacks slaves, so I cannot relate to the national heritage concepts introduced by society. I cannot readily go into a store and buy bandages which match my skin color, or other products which cater to my race. These are just a few examples of privileges which I am not awarded.

Although, my race does allow me some privileges. Being considered a minority, makes me eligible for more scholarhips. For example, when I enrolled at West Virginia University, I was selected to receive both the Storer African-American Scholarship and the Presidential Scholarship. A non-minority could only be offered a Presidential Scholarship which has a much higher selection criteria. As far as academics, I have been successful, in May 1997, I will graduate with a B.S. in Chemical Engineering. My academic success may very well correlate to my class standing.

My mother and father both work. Together they make six figures, therefore I am middle class. With my parents' salaries, I was able to get all the learning enrichment materials I needed. At an early age, I was enrolled in private school. I went to high school in the wealthiest area of Charleston, where educatation is top notch. My class allowed me many freedoms. In high school, I was in abundance of activities and could afford to pay the fees. Transportation was not a problem, I could always borrow my dad's Corvette or my mom's new Camaro Sport. I was socially accepted. As a result, my friends' parents are lawyers, doctors, and business managers, so I am very well connected

My class has allowed me the privilege of living in a safe neighborhood. My neighborhood is full of lawyers, doctors, engineers, and politicians, which is a privilege. One of my neighbors is a world-famous engineer who has helped me make a lot of connections in the scientific community. In the winter, the roads in my neighborhood are the first to be plowed. Any needed road repairs are made quickly. These are just a few privileges of being middle class.

Although being middle class, I have been oppressed, mostly due to internal oppression. Some blacks have said I was trying to be "white" because I went to a wealthy school, or spoke properly, or lived in a prominent neighborhood. The fact is, that trying to get ahead in life does not mean being "white". If that's the case, then being "black" means trying to fail. This is definitely a case of internalized oppression. What those negative people do not realize, is what you have to *have*, in order to *give*. "Black women have long seen the activist potential of education and have sought it as a cornerstone of community development – means of uplifting the race." In high school, I tutored weekly at the inner-city community center, and am now starting to tutor again. I have ran free cheer camps at the inner-city community centers. I gave free dance lessons to girls ages 8-12. I took the dance squad to competition two years and both years they placed. I know that the more I learn, the more I have to share with others. So, if learning means being "white" in the eyes of some people, then I guess I'll have to be just that.

My persistence of being involved and taking on challenges propagates throughout my life. My choice to pursue a Chemical Engineering degree is par for my competitive nature. Engineering is not a "traditional" field for women. The social constuction of gender does not establish women as intellectual scientific thinkers. The number of women in engineering is increasing, especially in Chemical Engineering. In my engineering group there are 13 guys and me. I am used to being a minority, that does not bother me, but at times, the guys' camaraderie does. Sometimes my classmates do not include me in their discussions (and sometimes I'd rather not know). The guys establish manliness through male bonding, which does not allow for female inclusion. "Many women science and engineering students feel isolated and perceive that they are resented by male students. Women are frequently interrupted in learning groups, and their contributions are often ignored by men. Women who are confident in science and engineering classrooms often elicit negative responses from their male peers." Being a minority, I must prove that I am just as good as my colleagues or even better.

Reflections of the Heart

    Depending on the setting, and the background of the people I interact with, I may experience privilege or oppression, or even both in the same instance. "Yes: race and class and gender remain as real as the weather. But what they must mean about the contact between two individuals is less obvious and, like the water, not predictable.

INSPIRED BY AN IMAGE

Who could you imagine yourself after????
Ask yourself this question.
Can you look into the reality mirror of Life
And see the image you want to be remembered
Most people would rather think they already have an image
Or shall we say and idea of Who, What, When and Where
They will be and they're pretty much satisfied
However, the Role Models and Wisdom Wizards of my time
Make me want to wonder back to the inspiring person's image
I would Love to identify with,
Is it a face of fullness, smiles, frowns, gladness, sadness?
Tears, wrinkles, smoothe, soft, delicate skin or
Rough, dry, cracked and irritated surface?
Look deep into the mirror
Tell me what you see
Are you Inspired by what time can tell?
Is it strong with Love or Weak and Frail?
I'm Inspired By Your Visage
But Most of All Your image!!!!!!

Gladine Pannell Bruer
8/8/2006

Reflections of the Heart
LITTLE FELLAS

My heart it yearns

My stomach churns

When I think about the Little Fellas

My face it smiles

With every mile

When I think of the Little Fellas

When I first met

The Little Fellas

My eyes they got to watch them grow

Through sun, rain, sleet, hell and snow

Through Summer, Winter, Fall and Spring

The Little Fella's into everything

Climb the counter, jump the fence

Growing each day, inch by inch

Still talking about The Little Fellas

As I watch the days, months and years go by

The Little Fellas make me Cry

Not from sadness but from joy

These Little Fellas

Are our Big Boys

All grown up and handsome too!

Ready for the world, What can they do?

Just about anything they desire.

Because we know they've got the power

Black, White, Rich or Poor

Reflections of the Heart

Life will open many doors
But no matter how high they Soar
Our Little Fellas
Go off to War
So as we wake to each new day
For the Little Fellas
WE WILL PRAY!!!!

Gladine Pannel Bruer
08/08/2006

BY CHANCE

By chance did you wake up today?
By chance did you give thanks and pray?
By chance are you in good health?
By chance is your life full of wealth?
By chance are you in control?
By chance can you see the writing Bold?
By chance have you rendered your soul?
By chance are you young or old?
By chance can you ask for forgivenesss?
If by chance the answer is yes
By chance you've passed the Lord's test
And Only
By chance!!!!!!

GPB
10-2006

A Cold Man in Your Day

As time passes me by
I can feel the chill
Days gone by – No big deal
As brisk and as cold as a winter breeze
A cold man in your day
I do believe
To deny, and say things
that really hurt
Memory brings them back in little spurts
The flouncing of the hussies pale
It's a wonder I didn't go to jail
A cold man in your day
No smile, no laughs, no time to play
A cold man you were
IN YOUR DAY!!!!!!

Gladine Pannell Bruer
10-2006

I Adore
by Brittany White

What did you do to me when you said, "Hi"
You made me happy and I almost cried
When you lied, I could have died
But I forgave you and you didn't say bye
I ask you why, why you stood by my side.

Why do you wanna be with me
You carved our names in a tree
Why can't I see what you need me to be
You say you love me more and more
You say I'm the only one you adore.

You trust me, I trust you
But sometimes your friends are such fools
Then you act around me so cool.
No matter what goes on between us
We never really fuss

You say you love me more and more
I'm the only one you adore
I say I love you more and more
We both love each other and adore

DAYS GONE BY

How often do you think of day's gone by?
Remembering visions and goals of success
Oh those were the days we loved the best
Days gone by as we look in the mirror –
Time shows only within thine eyes – the skin
Is not smooth – the lips they are wrinkled
The hair on one's head is just little sprinkles
Yes these all show The Days Gone by –
What now
That we have watched The Days Gone By –
What left
Can we salvage any of The Days Gone By?
Have all the Days been in vain?
Do they thoughts drive you insane?
Ask yourself the ultimate question
What did you do with your
Days Gone By?

Gladine Pannell Bruer

The Smile of an Empty Face

Look in the Mirror

The stare is long over due!

What do you see?

A face – An empty Face!

Is there a frown or a smile on this face?

Which would you like to see?

Frowns full of neglect and sorrow

Or

Smiles that will fill up the empty face?

Smiles fill the emptiness of a face.

By Gladine Pannel Bruer
1-2007
To ALL the empty faces in this world
God be your guide.

ARE YOU UNHAPPY?

Are you unhappy
Is your unhappiness due to space
Or are you blaming it on your race?
Are you unhappy with everyday life
Boredom, negativity, and strife?
Are your surroundings overwhelming
Full of darkness and misunderstanding?
Are you unhappy with the hand you were dealt?
Have you taken the time to see how other felt?
Is your health bad, are you homeless and sad?
Do you question where your next dollar is from?
Are you classified by the word BUM?
Did you get a chance to see the day start?
Can you hear the thump of your working heart?
If your answer is YES to the last two lines
The five before should be a sign
That in this life, you're doing Just Fine!!!
So why are you unhappy?????

By Gladine Pannell Bruer
1-2007
To all the unhappy people in this world
GOD BLESS.

Reflections of the Heart
RED'S DAUGHTER
BY CRYSTAL (ARMSTEAD) GOOD
2007

I am a blending
Of Rand
Of St. Albans

Of the City of Marigolds
to the HomeOf Randy Moss
Of low
Of middle and upper Kanawha incomes

A blending
Of black
Of white
Of "Tell em' you're American"
Of "West By God Virginia"

But in Affrilachia Of is not enough
You must be from somewhere,
You must belong to somebody.

Dunbar? Institute? Mt. Hop? Beckley?
You must be somebody's daughter.

Indeed

I be Red's daughter
Of the East End
Of Carte Street
Of courtyards with mixed flowers
I be Leones' granchildren by way
Of Charleston High

I be country, I be hip, I be hop, I be rock, I be soul and
often I try to be symphonic

Reflections of the Heart

I be in all the faces and places.
I be something new. I be something old,
Of again.

And, everyday, I be wondering whether to blend in or out
Of right
Of dead wrong

I be Red's daughter, black girl, white woman,
black woman, white girl
with a pink neck.

I be Harley riding, tractor pullin', I be
Of the white water.

I be singing country roads to let your shoulder lean–
Laughing with all the white boys, pimpin' my ride.
I am a blending
Of Rand
Of St. Albans
Of No Yes Ave.

A blending
Of fickle
Of fine
Of "that girl can't make up her mind"

I be Red's Daughter, one
Of a kind. I be Red's Daughter.

PASS YOU BY

When morning comes and you see the sky,
Don't let the day pass you by
When each breath taken is less than a try,
Don't let the moment pass you by.
When life you can look square in the eye,
Take this advise – don't pass it by,
Because when at last it's your day to sign,
All your life will not pass you by.

Gladine Pannell Bruer

LIFE

Breathing – smiling – laughing – Life you come so easy to me,
How can I hold on to you?
As a Human being – Life can be what you make it.
Happy – Satisfying – Cherished, consider what it means to you.
Life – you only get one chance.

Gladine Bruer

THE MOORE YOU WANT

The Moore you want is the more you will get
Because with Ethel you were a sure bet
Shooting straight from the hip
You gave her little or No lip
Kind, thoughtful and generous too.
Even on days when she had the Blues.
A wife, a mother, a sister and friend
Wish there were moore like her

Just for Ethel
Love Gla
6-2007

Reflections of the Heart

PAGES OF YOUR LIFE
(TAKEN FROM THE WORDLESS BOOK)

The Golden Page is heaven sent

The Holy Creator God is there in print
As we all know he loves us all
Small, medium, large or tall
As we all confess that we have sinned
The Lord helps us begin again
Because we all know in heaven No Sin!!!
So on to the Dark Page where we've all been

Sin as we know is Born within
Red is the page where this begins

Jesus, God's Perfect Son
Died, buried and rose again
Took the punishment for our sin
Thinking, saying and doing bad things
To God's strong heart, sadness it brings
God has a plan for you and me
He will be there to help thee
The Clean Page is all yours.

Admit you're a sinner–make him smile
Believe in the Lord with every mile
Choose God in your Life and you will Grow
Green as the grass we all know

Reflections of the Heart

Go to church regularly
Read your Bible whole heartedly
Obey and respect, that's his call
Witness his word to one and all
Last but not least, Day after Day
Stop and take the time to Pray
In regards to the Wordless Book

As God's child, you should be hooked
If you're going through pain and strife
Try making these Pages
A part of your LIFE

Gladine Pannell Bruer
3-19-3007

Reflections of the Heart

MS. HICKS
TO MOTHER HICKS (ONE OF MY MOTHERS IN CHRIST)
CHERISHING HER MEMORY ALWAYS

Remembering Ms. Hicks
She was one of my Picks
A woman of Truth
A woman of Strength
But you didn't dare take her The Length!!!
Because with her firmness
And Kind ways
Respect was due her
Each and every day
She stood for what's Right
And frowned on What's Wrong
A woman with a heart
True and Strong
Always making one feel that
They were a part
Rememberiing her is so good for the heart
Remembering Ms. Hicks
A mentor and friend
Remembering her smile
From beginning to end
This poem I dedicate
To Ms. Hicks
A woman who will always be
One of my favorite Picks

By Gladine Pannell Bruer
6-2007

BABY BOY!

This poem is to my Baby Boy
Who looks at life as one big Toy
That's Okay – I understand
But you're all grown up, so be a Man
Take care of what is Precious to you
Tyler, Avery, and number 3 – Pooh
Let's not forget old mom and dad
Dee or Mike that would be so sad
Take care and remember your legacy
And how you will want it to be
Bad or Good, Dark or Bright, False or True
Baby Boy it's all up to you
Respect and Honor – Are you due these things?
Because this Baby Boy is what a legacy Bring

Love Mom
Forever to My Baby Boy (Carl L. Bruer, Jr.)

FAMILY

What does the word Family mean to you?
To me Family Means
F-forever-limitless time-Like God All The Time
A-Awesome-a remarkable and outstanding group
M-Memories–storing of the good & bad
I-Inevitable–the unavoided people in our Lives
L-Love & Loyalty–warm personal attachment
Y-Youthful days remembered–yesterdays!
This my brothers and Sisters is
FAMILY!!!!!!

www.ingramcontent.com/pod-product-compliance
Lightning Source LLC
LaVergne TN
LVHW050026080526
838202LV00069B/6936